A Gardener
on the Moon

A Gardener
on the Moon

Carole Giangrande

QUATTRO BOOKS

The publication of *A Gardener on the Moon* has been generously supported by the Canada Council for the Arts.

Canada Council   Conseil des Arts
for the Arts   du Canada

Cover art: Diane Mascherin
Cover design: Diane Mascherin
Typography: Grey Wolf Typography

Library and Archives Canada Cataloguing in Publication

Giangrande, Carole
    A gardener on the moon / Carole Giangrande.

ISBN 978-1-926802-05-3

    I. Title.

PS8563.I24G37 2010   C813'.54   C2010-902017-0

Published by Quattro Books
P.O. Box 53031, Royal Orchard Postal Station
10 Royal Orchard Blvd.,
Thornhill, ON, L3T 3C0
www.quattrobooks.ca

Printed in Canada

For Brian

Language is the only homeland.
— Czeslaw Milosz

I

THEY WERE MARRIED ONLY two years when one night, after Pierre had sheltered in the comfort of her body, Marie-Hélène touched him and said, "Have you ever wondered if you could live alone again?"

The words fell into his ear and shivered there with the sweetness of something long forbidden. Pierre answered, "If I had to, I'd become a *coureur de bois*. I would never return from the woods. Better yet, I'd farm. I'd do whatever would help me forget you." He looked into her dark eyes which were at that moment impenetrable. "And you?" he asked.

"I'd have no choice," she answered. "I'd have to stay here. Every day I'd see you in our children."

Thérèse was a toddler by then; Danielle an infant. Pierre loved them both and he never forgot the thoughtlessness of his answer that night, the sad truth he'd spoken from the heart. He knew Marie-Hélène had understood him well. She'd tested him with a lover's riddle, asking him to confess the thing he loved above all others. And so he had.

Eighteen years later, Marie-Hélène was struggling with cancer. Her body had been under ruthless siege, and it felt to Pierre as if the sickness were his also. Now they were living apart, and from time to time, he drove into Montreal for a Sunday visit. As ill and insubstantial as she'd been, Marie-Hélène appeared to be at least as well as Pierre. She seemed to inhabit a place of repose, its light subdued, its curtains drawn against his eyes. Alone she drank from the well of solace she'd offered him for all the years of their marriage, and after a year of hope and forbearance, she'd begun to strengthen. "*Je vais vivre*, I'm going to live," she said to Pierre. "Don't be afraid."

They celebrated her forty-fifth birthday in the chill late November of 1970. In Montreal, it had been an autumn of trouble — kidnappings, arrests, a cabinet minister shot dead in the trunk of a car. "*Je reste calme*," said Marie-Hélène, as she arranged flowers and refused to watch TV. Danielle was late for their *soirée* and Pierre got up, stared out the front window, sat down, got up again.

"She'll be all right," said his wife. "She's bringing a cake."

Pierre calmed down, understanding the strength of that remark, its gentle conviction that everyday things more often went right than wrong. It was this belief that was keeping her alive, Pierre felt sure. She'd insisted she'd get well, and she'd surrounded herself with friends and relatives, people who laughed as he did not.

The door opened and in came Danielle, out of breath.

"*Pardon*, the traffic's bad. *Bonne fête*." She kissed her mother, brought the cake into the kitchen, then hugged Pierre.

His daughter resembled Marie-Hélène when she was young — her sleek dark hair, her eyes composed and tranquil, hiding a strength of will he couldn't fathom. She clothed herself in an odd assortment of headbands and beadwork, an Indian-cotton tunic thrown over her sweater, her jeans embroidered with flowers and butterflies. There was a sweet lopsidedness to her collection of mismatched garments, and it touched Pierre, as if she were a toddler playing grown-up, tripping around in her mother's high-heeled shoes. Marie-Hélène turned to him.

"Danielle has been to Massachusetts," she said.

"*Oui, elle me l'a dit.*"

Danielle had driven through St.-Jean-de-Sapins on her way home for Thanksgiving, and she'd stopped by to tell him where she'd been. A school project, *des recherches,* she'd said, proud that her English was good enough for the library in Boston. She'd sniffed out the town of Greenbanks, gleaning the name from her father's scant talk. He shrugged. *Sa petite Danielle* wanted to be a journalist. She was grown now, eighteen years old, after all.

His daughter went into the kitchen, returning with the cake, the candles lit. Pierre couldn't remember what birthday rhyme they sang, only that the words caught in his throat and he couldn't finish the song. Marie-Hélène blew out the candles. *What had she wished for?* he wondered. Long life, *bien sûr.* Yet her breath made the room dark and tossed away the stars.

II

HOW DARK HIS LIFE had been before he knew Marie-Hélène.

When he'd returned to the U.S. in 1945, he was Pete LeBlanc of Greenbanks, Massachusetts. On that particular day, he'd fallen into the French of his youth, thanking his mother for his favourite dish, his first good meal in years. *J'ai rêvé de cette tourtière. I dreamed about this grub, no kidding.* He hadn't spoken his parents' tongue in the service, and it seemed as distant as his childhood visits to *grand-père* in Quebec, to the village his family left before his birth. He remembered teasing his mom and dad, telling them that by the time he came back from the war, he wouldn't know *tu* from *tout.*

Now his father looked amused. *"Qu'est-ce que tu as fait durant la guerre?"* he asked. "Study French?" Pete smiled, and his tongue simmered with words as he ate, as if the spicy *tourtière* was prodding him to speak. His mother filled his plate again, but he hadn't eaten like this in years and he had no room for more.

Yet the food stirred him, and in the coolness of this late October day, Pete could reach out and feel with his hand the frost and cold on the edge of memory. He let his mind stretch and reach and bend itself back to a farm outside Saint-Charles-sur-Richelieu, not because of nostalgia (he couldn't remember the real place), but because it meant the comfort of a cool winter after the tropical dread of the war. He closed his eyes, telling himself how sane a thing it was to feel on his skin the steam of some imagined *grand-mère*'s kitchen. Yet when he looked at his plate again, he couldn't eat.

Pete got up to leave. He told them he was tired, that he had to sleep. His father took his arm as if he were an invalid and led him to his room. When Pete said goodnight, he gazed into the man's eyes and saw how disheartened he was, as tired as any soldier.

"I never thought I'd see you again," his dad said. He looked as if he'd been weeping, as if the long wait had bruised his face with sorrow. It was as if nothing, not even the presence of his missing son, could undo what he had suffered in his absence.

"Didn't they tell you anything?" Pete asked.

"The Red Cross knew you were alive." His father paused. "Lorraine did, too."

Pete didn't answer.

When his father left him alone, he forgot where he was. He felt as if he were lost again on an island in the Philippines, in the country north of Bataan. Yet moments later, he realized that he'd have to find his way home again, that he couldn't avoid

Lorraine's unhappiness. He remembered how he'd longed for her, how he ended up pushing her out of his head as if she'd been a dying captive in the heat of that long and terrible march, a victim he couldn't stop to pity. His best friend Allan was her brother, and years ago the three of them were pals. Before he and his buddy left for the war, they sat down with Lorraine, knocked off a bottle of scotch and swore they'd live to celebrate each other's fiftieth birthdays. "At your place," Allan said to him. "Yours and Lorrie's. In 1971, our kids will be as old as we are now." They wrote it on paper and signed it.

Lorraine would want to know how Allan died.

Home in autumn, well past V-J Day, he was grateful to have missed the streamers and champagne, joyrides and lindy-hopping, kisses from the girls. Words deserted him even when he saw his parents. "I understand," said his father. "You're home," his mother told him, as if she were waking him from sleep. Pete said how much he'd missed them, how grateful he was for their prayers. After that, he was silent, having said everything there was to say.

He could never talk about the prison camp, or how he'd learned about Lorraine and his child. Her letter had reached him days before he and Allan were captured by the Japanese. Poor Lorrie — her parents would have sent her to an aunt in Boston or New York or Montreal. Only there was no aunt — there never was. Lorraine would have been confined to a home for girls in trouble and made to feel ashamed of herself. They would have taken the baby away from her.

They'd both had misery enough.

Alone in his room, Pete stared at the family photos on his bureau, his four brothers and sisters, three of them living, all of them much older than himself: a priest in Rome, a cloistered nun, a married woman in California. He felt astonished that their photographs were here, as if in his internment he'd neglected them as well as Lorraine, as if he had no right to cast his eyes on these remote and kindly strangers. Missing was a brother, four years old, drowned in the Merrimac River a week before Pete's birth. In the child's memory, his parents gave Pete the middle name of Étienne. He'd resented that, as if they'd made him bear the weight of his brother's death. As it turned out, the name was too foreign for America. He shrugged it off, yet his muscles felt weary, haunted by the burden of a ghost.

Tired, he went to bed, but hearing the last of the kitchen sounds, he drifted into memories of shouts and gunfire, and the senseless calm of the night made him afraid. He felt choked and smothered by the terrible fear that his life had broken along cracks that couldn't be mended. Words would never mean anything again. They had collapsed under the rock-heavy burden of memory and horror and they were bloodied, like everything else. He had no idea how he was going to live with this.

Upon his return, his mother gave him a photograph of Lorraine taken during the war — a factory girl with her platinum curls tucked under a bandanna, the rest of her hidden in mannish clothes. In the picture, she's smiling, a forced *say cheese* kind of smile. She must have been exhausted from hammering and riveting, but that wouldn't have explained the look in her eyes, shadowed and empty, as if she were tired of gazing at the world. His Lorrie had always been as pretty as a seashell, her eyes a bluebird's colour, a shape *all hills and valleys,* as he used to say, his hands moulding the air. She'd won a prize once, singing on the radio, her bright voice heard across America. Pete had helped her rehearse for the broadcast, and he'd run through her song on the piano. "Someone To Watch Over Me," maybe that was it.

He couldn't remember.

When he called her, she welcomed him home with a weary voice. He invited her out to a movie, then bought her flowers and a box of chocolates, but he felt uneasy with simple pleasures, unsure of the contours of a world where these things were ordinary, a world where he no longer lived. It was a clear autumn night, and he glanced upward with the same eyes that had looked at the pale and glaring heat of a tropical sky. He remembered parachutes blooming open at the war's end with a God-sent hail of tinned meat, fish, bread, and candy, and he could still feel his body crying out with hunger as it did then. Clutching the chocolates, he rang the bell.

Before him stood a wan girl, her hair as tired as broomstraw. "Petey," she said, and he was shaking so hard he had to put the gifts down. He held her in his arms and kissed the lids of her eyes and then her lips.

"Lorrie, gal," he whispered.

He felt awkward with her tenderness, knowing she felt the same in his embrace. His was the wrong shape to soften the hollow inside her, and she wasn't sturdy enough to flesh out his gauntness. How strange it felt, the gentle touch of hands, of lips, the two of them searching with their bodies for the warmth of bodies remembered, for a time that had vanished. They were like tenants who'd lived in better places, now reduced to poverty, trying their best to adjust to shabbier surroundings. He felt her eyes on him, and he found it unbearable, meeting her gaze.

"Sweet Pete, we'll need to feed you some," she said.

"You're looking real good," he answered, knowing the minute he said it that he shouldn't have because it wasn't true. Lorrie's eyes were vast with suffering. She took the flowers and arranged them in a vase.

"You're being nice, Pete."

"Lorrie?"

"Huh?"

"I don't know what to say."

She put a finger to his lips. "There's nothing to say."

They went to the movies but Pete couldn't recall what film they saw. *We had a child,* he kept thinking. No, questions would hurt too much. He felt the touch of her finger on his lips; she didn't want to talk. Four years had passed. He hadn't thought he'd live through the siege of Bataan, and then he was taken prisoner and he couldn't write to her. He felt just as reluctant to speak about the past as she did, just as fearful of the high tide of grief. After the movie he took her hand and walked her home along the river bank.

"I know you had it rough," he said.

"You, too."

Pete kicked a pebble, sent it rolling down the bank. They walked along in silence. "You don't feel bad?" he asked.

"I miss my brother."

Pete didn't answer. He could feel Lorraine huddled inside herself, and it troubled him that they were each thinking different thoughts, lost in sufferings they couldn't share. They looked out at the river, and he found himself thinking of his own brother Étienne, the lost child who drowned before his birth, whose poor name got wedged between Pete and LeBlanc like a bomb victim pinned between a fallen rafter and the floor. Long ago he'd told Lorraine that he wanted to name their first child for his brother, in order to ease his parents' sorrow. Now Allan had been lost also, and one day Lorraine would name a child for him. This naming, he knew, would never end. There had been a war and the names of the dead were wreckage floating to the surface of the world. *Those names find us,* thought Pete. *They wash up from their graves. They will not sleep.*

"Do you remember the tree that Allan planted?" Lorraine asked.

Pete was startled from his reverie. Once on Arbor Day, in a world long gone, Allan had planted a beech tree in a Greenbanks park.

"Uh-huh," he said.

"The town's going to put a plaque on it."

I buried Allan, dug his grave, tossed lime on his face, threw another body over his. Days later he floated up in the ground-water. Or maybe I imagined it was him.

"Pete?"

"That's nice. The tree, I mean."

She took his arm and walked him away from the river.

They tried to sleep together and couldn't. Again and again, Pete saw in her face the prison camp, barbed wire, Allan near death. He couldn't escape the look of him in Lorraine's eyes, the sound of his friend's voice insisting that he eat, that he take some of his rice gruel ration, not real food at all. *I'm not gonna make it, Pete. Go on, eat up.* Ravenous, he took what Allan gave him until he saw that his eyes were shut and that he was too feverish to care how much Pete took from him. *Poor Allan.* He felt the weight of him in Lorraine's touch, the man he couldn't afford to pity.

Too much has happened, dear Lorrie, that I don't know how to fix.

Wanting refuge, Pete went to visit relatives in Canada. He felt at peace in his parents' ancestral home, and there he made the decision to begin his life again, to settle in the province of Quebec and claim a language in which nothing unspeakable had happened to him. He had discovered a place where he wanted to study, a college south of Montreal run by Trappist monks. Having almost perished from hunger, he'd decided to train as an agronomist, to help farmers raise their crops, to own a small farm of his own one day. He told Lorraine his plans.

"Life's made a mess of us," she said.

"Nuh-uh. You're headed for Hollywood," he told her.

"I'm too old."

"Go on. You have your whole life ahead." Pete touched her cheek. He could feel light coming through her skin, light on the tips of his fingers wet with her crying. She pulled away, wiped her face dry with her handkerchief, found her compact and began to powder her nose.

"We're both too old," she said.

Twenty-four years old, you call that old? he thought. Except that she was right.

"Lorrie, I hate this fucking world."

Pete opened a bottle of whiskey and poured two drinks. He lit Lorraine's cigarette. The smoke curled upward, slow and lazy as a cat's tail while she strolled back and forth, the sound of her heels emphatic on the floor. Her hair was coiffed, netted in a tight, sleek roll, and she wore a short wool jacket, a skirt cut to the knee. She was dressed as he'd never seen her, as if she were about to quit a tiresome, deluded life. This was a new Lorraine, slouching in a model's pose, blowing smoke through a bright, hard O of cherry lips. Pete thought of the cigarette ad, the one with the gorgeous movie stars. *Who was the blonde, Veronica Lake? At Home and Over There, It's Chesterfields.* Only Lorraine didn't smile like a movie star. She didn't look at him.

"A lousy world," she answered.

"Yeah," said Pete. "I know what's what."

Lorraine didn't flinch at his bitterness. She lifted her glass. "Here's to real life," she said.

"Love is impossible in this world," he replied. With a shrug, he tossed back his drink, then lit a cigarette, letting it dangle from his mouth. He enjoyed his lassitude, the tough, knowing sound of his words. He poured another round.

"War vets, us two," said Lorraine.

Their glasses clinked, again and again.

He left Lorraine, moved to Quebec and became Pierre LeBlanc, enrolling as a student at the Agricultural Institute in the town of Oka, south of Montreal. Silence had drawn him to this stone-gray seminary, to its dairy farm known for fine cheese, to its barnyard and granary, to the tranquillity of its orchards and stands of sugar maple. For four years he resided there, absorbed by his studies, but the school itself, so modern in every respect, only intensified his yearning for an older world, one that had existed long before the horrors he'd witnessed had upended his life. He was envious of the monks, who went about their farming tasks in silence, who left the teaching to lay instructors as if mindful of their own superior calling, as if knowing the incompleteness of whatever words might say.

Yet he did not have a monastic vocation or the gift of prayerful silence, or even faith. He had only his years as a prisoner of war, and the fading memory of his first love.

Even so, Pierre managed to make friends, and on weekends they'd go into Montreal, to a university campus club, where after a drink or two, he'd play the piano — blues and jazz and the *chansons* of Edith Piaf, songs that allowed the pain of love and regret to dance on his fingertips and nowhere else. He'd remember Lorraine, how he'd helped her rehearse for the contest she'd won on the radio, but he wouldn't touch the kit bag of sentimental ditties from the war, wouldn't upset himself by playing "Now Is the Hour" or "I'll Be Seeing You" or anything by the Andrews Sisters or Vera Lynn.

His was casual and quiet playing, nothing that should have attracted anyone's attention. He enjoyed his disguise, lost in his repertoire of Parisian *chansons*, hidden in the smoke of his dangling cigarette. His friends loved his nonchalance. They'd lean against the piano, singing along, shouting *bravo, Pierre! encore!* as they clapped for a man who wasn't even there.

One evening, someone found him.

"You play very well," she said. Her name was Marie-Hélène Demers, and she was also a student.

"Do you play?" he asked.

She smiled at him. "It would not be as entertaining."

"C'mon, play."

Reluctant at first, she played part of a Mozart sonata. Pierre told her it was beautiful. He had no idea how Mozart was supposed to sound, but he could sense her gravity, the calm, ineffable pull of it on the slight particle of matter that he was. She told him she'd lived her early life in France and he could feel the distance of the place in her. Its serenity was mapped in the planes and angles of her face, in her straight black hair in a chignon, in her composure that was not in any way American, in her body's silence, as if it were a place of contemplation. She asked him where he learned French. Her eyes were calm ponds and he could smell lilies and the heat of summer.

"I spoke it with my folks," he said.

"Vous êtes canadien?"

"My parents were. That's why I came here."

"For your studies?"

"I wanted to come home," he said.

"Where is home?"

He didn't know where, and it surprised him that he'd mentioned it. He supposed he meant his grandparents' farm near Saint-Charles-sur-Richelieu, but he wasn't sure. It had been his constant thought in the Philippines, *Christ, I miss home.* English words in desperate times, words that became the strain and pull of his body on the prisoners' long march when he never thought beyond the work of putting one foot down, and then another. Home was the wish of his emaciated flesh that every step would take him closer to the end of his ordeal. Pete lowered his eyes. He could feel Marie-Hélène, her compassion, the gentle turning away of her gaze, as if she were pulling a sheet over a corpse.

"I don't know where home is," he said.

"Is that because you were in the war?"

"Maybe."

"My parents, too," she said. "They long for France."

Marie-Hélène spoke the words as if she were about to take him on a long and solemn journey. He felt mesmerized as she put her hands on the keyboard and began to play. The melody was strange, hundreds of years old, she told him, one her parents loved. "They're Renaissance scholars," she said. "Don't try to understand the French." She sang along, her voice almost too soft to hear.

Estans assis aux rives aquatiques
De Babylon plorions melancoliques

"*Vous comprenez?* 'By the rivers of Babylon, we sat and wept.'"

Pierre said yes, he understood.

"You have fine hands," she told him. "You should play more."

"You know what I wanna do with 'em?" he asked.

She met his eyes with a curious look.

"Farm," said Pierre. He waited for a cultivated laugh. None came.

"*Oui, je comprends,*" she said. "My parents have a garden. They, too find consolation in the soil."

Pierre lit a cigarette, nervous with an impulse to talk as he hadn't done in years. He thought of carrying on about his folks who'd been farmers in Quebec. Maybe he could add that toward the end of the war he was allowed to garden in a showcase prison, that he became adept at small-scale farming in odd climatic zones.

"I'm with Voltaire," he said. *"Il faut cultiver votre jardin."*

"Oui, Pierre. But Candide turned his back on the world."

Pierre ground out his cigarette. "Forget the world."

"And if you cannot?"

"I can," he said. "I went to war in English."

"So?"

"I don't speak it anymore. I don't even think in it."

She laughed. *"C'est impossible. C'est ta langue."*

"I don't know anyone who died in French," he said.

Marie-Hélène grew still. *"Oui,"* she said. "I understand."

"So finish your song," said Pierre.

Marie-Hélène began to play again.

She called him Pierre, and he became dizzy with pleasure at the thought of his old self dissolving into the shape and touch of her hands. He began to feel as if he were no more than a word, as if the French language were a tongue uttering him. No, more than that. Her language was a river in flood over dry land, and it sated his thirst. Marie-Hélène called forth serenity, as if at the centre of herself was prayer, a still pool of silence. *Even if you don't talk,* she said, *je t'entends.*

Carole Giangrande

Montreal
15 October 1947

Chère Marie-Hélène,

.... two years have passed, yet I still can't bring myself to talk about the war. Everyone suffered but what we went through was unspeakable. It's a paradox, that speech should feel like a defilement of those who suffered, but speech is a civilized thing, and Bataan was not. Memory is terrible — it distorts and invents, it lets us hold on to our sanity, and yet what is it but a continuous act of destruction, the final creation of a thing that never happened? Leave the truth to God, who remembers all.

Let me write down what memory does. In school I had a friend named Allan, but in my mind he's become Alain. He was the brother of a girl I used to love. His surname was Durocher, pronounced the same as the famous baseball player's. An American name, but now I think of it in the French way. He was rocher, *rock, while I was born* Pierre, *a stone. Alain was a big man with sawdust hair and dark eyes that smacked into yours, like an engine coupling with a boxcar.*

He was also a serious man. Alain wanted to enter politics, to go to Washington. He wanted to conduct the Boston Symphony and to write about the theatre for Le Monde. *His French was perfect. On the march from Bataan, he gave me water, the last he had. He threw his body over mine and he burst apart with fire. He dropped dead of sunstroke while forced to march to San Fernando Pampagna in the hills. He was shot dead for not doing what his captors ordered. He didn't understand Japanese. It is possible that in the end, I saw him drown.*

Can't you see what a scavenger I am, picking through the rubble? All of it happened and none of it did. It is defilement to crush such rotten fruit into words. I will not speak about the victims of Bataan. Let me treat the unspeakable as holy ground.

Do you understand, that I no longer know what happened?

III

OVER TWENTY YEARS HAD passed, and even now, he didn't know.

Marie-Hélène had consoled him. *In time, words will come,* she'd written back, but they never did. Instead marriage came, and with it, the solace of their children.

"Bravo, maman!" said Danielle.

She turned on the light, jarring Pierre out of his reverie. Now he watched his daughter as she handed her mother a knife to cut her cake, a white-frosted *gâteau aux carottes*. He couldn't imagine what on earth a cake made with vegetables would taste like. *C'est organique,* said his daughter, who worried that her father, an *agronome*, was instructing farmers to spray their crops. He tried the cake, found it delicious, thanked her for introducing him to something new. Then he gave Marie-Hélène his gift.

As he did, he caught his daughter's saddened look. *Poor Danielle*, he thought. It was hard for her, that he'd moved out.

On top of that, knowing he didn't want the past disturbed, she'd quite by accident tracked it down in Boston. Now Danielle found it hard to look at him, to be in the same room. She collected the dishes, then excused herself.

Marie-Hélène opened her gift, took the crimson scarf from its box and draped it around her neck so that it set off her black hair and the translucent whiteness of her skin. It seemed to Pierre as if her face were a lantern, its light casting out the shadows of her illness. She stood up, looked in the mirror, turned the scarf one way, then another. "*Bien,* that suits me well," she said. "I'll wear it for an evening out." She walked to the piano, then sat down.

"I wish you good health," he said.

"You don't look well, Pierre."

Or maybe she thought he looked unkempt. It was the farm that had done that, his leave of absence from his job and proper dress, his three months' living at their summer place. His hands were rough and humble with work; his hair had grown white and as long as a youth's. She'd told him once that his eyes were eloquent, a blue of sombre tales, the colour of the stained glass in the great cathedral of Chartres. He wondered what she saw there now.

"I am well," he said at last. "I work hard."

"You're alone, I take it."

"*Comme un moine.* Like a monk."

There was a small florist's bouquet on the piano, marigolds and asters. Pierre looked away.

"You noticed that," she said.

"I'm surprised you'd allow it in the house," he replied.

"Her niece brought it. The child still comes for lessons." She paused. "You'll remember that every week when I was ill, that little girl brought flowers from her Aunt Nicole."

Pierre turned his back, then stared out the window. Nicole, a woman who, for a short while, had obsessed him — fair-haired, short-skirted, robust with good health and life. He remembered how desperate he'd felt during his wife's illness, how frantic Nicole had made him feel, as if life itself were beyond his reach until one afternoon, after she dropped off her niece from the lesson, he followed her home and up the stairs to her apartment. Realising that she'd offer no resistance, he'd walked in the door, turned her around and kissed her, surprised to find her so ready to receive him that his mind shut down and his flesh resented Marie-Hélène for what she could no longer give, for bringing death into the house, for defiling the shelter of their marriage. *Whenever I set foot in your home, I sense what you're missing in life,* said Nicole with a shrug. Struck by this remark, Pierre blamed Marie-Hélène — not with words, but with anxiety that wanted release from her illness, from this caustic thing that had corroded the bond between them. Yet Marie-Hélène remained calm and brave, and in the face of this, he felt confronted by his own cowardice, knowing it was not the first time in his life he'd run away from a woman in desperate straits. *Un vrai cochon,* he'd call himself when yearning overcame him, when he'd seek out Nicole.

The woman grew tired of his self-loathing. *Is it hate you want?* she asked. *Punishment?* His face still stung with the hard slap that awoke him from his trance.

Recalling this, Pierre glanced at the bouquet again, but he couldn't meet his wife's gaze.

He would always be sorry for the loss of many things that wouldn't return, including her trust. Gone were those Saturdays when she practiced scales and taught Mozart while he dug up the soil under her window, ripping out weeds and suckers to the counterpoint of a Bach fugue, shoving his hands into the muck with the fury of a desperate, hungry man who (his daughters said) *peut jardiner sur la lune*, could garden on the moon, so luxuriant were the vines he grew, peas and tomatoes and *haricots verts*. He'd never spoken as he gardened, seized as he was by the impulse to dig and plant. His quietness had bloomed with a dazzle of poppies bright as circus tents, so that even the deepest silence was redeemed with wild, graceful hollyhocks, sunflowers vast with bees.

He'd betrayed this. He must have been mad.

"I have much to think about," he said at last.

Marie-Hélène's voice was gentle. "Which is why you need time alone," she said.

"*Oui.* I always wanted to farm."

"Next spring you can help me," she replied. "The garden will need work by then." Marie-Hélène walked to the window and glanced at the spot where the tulip bulbs lay buried. In the silence, he heard what she used to say: *Throw in some moondust to keep off the squirrels, mon cher.* She'd never again talk with such endearment.

"I'll do the spring cleanup," said Pierre.

The phone rang. From the kitchen, he could hear Danielle. "*Allô?* Oh, hel-lo!"

His ears were pelted with English words. It would be Thérèse, he thought, calling from San Francisco. French had been the rule at home, and Danielle had lowered her voice so that she could practise English with her sister. Moments later, the girls were speaking French again. Danielle asked her mother to pick up the phone.

Merci, ma chérie, je vais bien, said Marie-Hélène, and her eyes sparkled. Yes, she'd received her gift, a beautiful woven shawl, made by a daughter who was studying art, and Pierre could hear the happy chatter of a faraway voice, its thin, piping telephone sounds like raucous little birds. He'd never been able to understand how women found so much to talk about, or how so much casual *bavardage* could bring them joy. He felt a pang of loneliness, as if he spoke a language no one knew.

"Would you like to speak to Thérèse?" asked Marie-Hélène. She left the room.

Pierre took the phone. *"Comment tu t'en passes, Thérèse?"*

"I'm well, and I really love my classes."

Thérèse was proud of her English and she spoke it well, but he'd always question her in French, worried that she'd lose the language in America.

"Il fait beau là?" he continued.

"The weather's out of sight, dad."

He puzzled over the expression, but from her tone of voice, it sounded fine.

"Ici il fait froid," he continued.

"You can have the cold. I'm glad I live in California, frankly."

He'd already told Thérèse that he and her mother had decided to part — no, he'd written her, feeling too ashamed to tell her much. It occurred to him later that he'd never had a lot to say to poor Thérèse in either French or English. She was much closer to her mother, who by now would have told her the truth about him.

He felt as if he were talking to a ghost. He heard her voice.

"Are you still there, dad?"

"Oui. Je suis ici.

"Can I speak to mom again?"

After she got off the phone, Marie-Hélène sat down at the piano and began to play. Pierre listened, relaxing in his old chair, just as he'd done in happier times. His wife was playing a piece she'd be teaching once again, *grace à Dieu* — Brahms or Haydn, he hadn't the knowledge to tell them apart. Yet the music stirred him, so that he imagined himself in spring, tidying her garden, digging craters under her window, unearthing fossils and moon-rocks, flowers in the dry land on which he stood. Her playing made him feel like that. It stirred hope in him, but in what, he wasn't certain.

It was getting late, and Pierre had an hour's drive back to the farm. He went to say goodnight to Danielle. "Are you staying over?" he asked her.

She looked surprised. "I can, papa."

"*Maman* is alone. You would be good company for her."

"You're leaving then?"

"I cannot stay."

"You could," she whispered.

"Non, ma petite."

Marie-Hélène stepped into the room. "I will be fine alone," she said.

Pierre said goodnight to them and stepped outside. Above his head, clouds darkened the Montreal sky, and he shuddered, remembering that only a month ago, terrorists were here, along with roadblocks, the army and police, and here he was, ex-prisoner of war, leaving his wife and daughter to cope alone with a city under siege. He looked up at the streaks of cloud that blinked out the stars as if they were embers from a lost fire, from Allan, left to die in the camp, and he could feel ash in his mouth, a savage mountainside from long ago where nothing grew, where there was no planting anything, no hope.

You have no right to get lost in the past, he thought. He realised he'd been lost too long in a fog of illusion through which he'd drifted for years, back and forth across Rue Ste. Catherine and Rue St. Denis or Sherbrooke Street. It was all the same. Montreal had been home to him as an oxygen tent was home to a very sick man. He'd never grown to love it. He preferred the farm and admired Marie-Hélène, a woman who, having rescued him, was brave enough to fight for her life and proud enough to reject his company in front of Danielle. Yes, she'd be better off without him, at least for now.

One day he'd return to her in gardening clothes, to dig and to dig until he grew too old to remember either the indignity he'd done to his marriage or the happiness he'd thrown away. It was fair punishment. For some reason, he felt better, knowing that.

Because of Danielle, he'd heard from Lorraine, and her letter arrived the day before the birthday *soirée*. He'd gone into the *dépanneur* in Saint-Jean-de-Sapins. Gaetan was standing behind the counter, his tart smile curled like a shaving of rind. The man reached into his cubbyhole and handed him his mail.

"It's there a week now. *Pauvre* Marie-Hélène."

Pierre glanced at the envelope. "It's not my wife's writing."

He saw puzzlement in Gaetan's eyes. *Has he a lover?* The man would wonder — he knew the family from summers past, and he'd no doubt observed that Pierre had been three months in the country without Marie-Hélène. *Un homme derangé, vraiment fou* — the guy had to be nuts, he'd think. A sweet wife and two lovely girls, and why would he live apart from them?

Pierre took the letter, thanked him and left.

It was from the States.

Dear Pete, Lorraine wrote. *It's been many years since we've been in touch, but your daughter Danielle made a trip to Boston while doing some research for a school project on her American background, which I gather you aren't too chatty about. She went to the cenotaph in Greenbanks, and found the tree that Allan planted, with his name on the plaque. The library was right across the street and someone there knew me and remembered us (can you believe it?). They sent her here to the library on Boylston Street in Beantown, the film desk. There I was. Small world, huh? And aren't I lucky I still understand French (even though I don't speak it), because your kid tells me that* anglais *is a no-no* chez toi. *By the way, it was a pleasure to meet Danielle (not to mention a real shockeroo), and that prodded me to dig up a reminder of a reunion we had planned with my brother, long ago. Which is why I'm writing. I'm coming to Montreal for a wedding next summer. How would it be if I took a day and drove out to see you? Allan would have loved that.*

Stapled to the letter was a photocopy of a note dated June 15th, 1941. *In celebration of our friendship, we pledge to meet and drink a toast at the age of fifty years. We hope for nice weather, a long hike and a picnic with plenty of booze. To this agreement, we sign our names and set our drinking glasses.* Next to the words were three overlapping rings and their signatures, his, Lorraine's and Allan's.

Mon Dieu, he saw their faces as they were when they were young. Then he wondered why some parts of life drifted off, forgotten, while others boomeranged and came back shrieking through time, gathering velocity like bullets. *One that has your name on it,* they said during the war.

He sat down and wrote to her. *Yes, Lorraine. You are welcome to come.*

IV

WINTER PASSED AND SPRING came, and Pierre turned the soil on his small patch of land in the Richelieu River valley. He'd bought the place years ago — a farm southeast of his parents' village in Quebec, just a short drive to Mont-Saint-Hilaire, where he used to take the girls and their mother for hikes. It wasn't the best land, some of it rough and hilly. Even so, Pierre had decided to seed it with crops.

Knowing he worked for the province, some of the local farmers would seek out his advice. Pierre found this more satisfying than phoning out the same information from his desk in Montreal. He decided that when his leave was up, he'd apply for the job of *agronome* for the eastern region of Montérégie where he now resided, where he expected to live for the rest of his life.

This year's crops were in the ground — lettuce and spinach, peas and tomatoes, carrots, potatoes and beans. There was a small grove of maples for tapping in early spring, and he'd made himself a sugar shack, a root cellar, a tool shed, a compost bin. Pierre enjoyed the rhythm of physical work, and it deepened in him a yearning for solitude. Alone, he tried to understand the collapse of good sense two years before when Marie-Hélène was diagnosed with cancer. Now he wondered if he'd ever loved her, or if he'd used her to escape his suffering. He asked himself if he'd been much of a husband, or if he'd only slept like a child in her arms.

He was fifty years old, and even though he was trained in scientific farming, he still felt it a wondrous thing that the hard clay soil would yield to his tractor, would soften with shovelfuls of compost and manure, would be open to the grace of sun and rain. Even as Marie-Hélène struggled with cancer, even as he suffered his confusion of the spirit, the ground would have none of it and crops began to grow. Cheered by this, he started to enjoy his quiet life. It had consoled him to think about turning the soil for Marie-Hélène in spring, as if his care for her garden might ease the sorrow between them. Mindful of his need for solitude, he began to feel some kinship with those bearded young men and long-haired women from the city who'd buy some land and ask his advice, who wanted to grow organic alfalfa and bean sprouts. He tried to imagine farming with horses as his *grand-père* did, stopping at noon for the Angelus bells, erecting a wooden cross in his field, but he knew it was too late for that. He was a modern, educated man who had not been faithful to religion, who had nothing left of it but gratitude for his life and the knowledge of his human frailty. Content, he farmed as everyone else farmed, minding Danielle's remarks about the sprays.

Only now he hoped never to return to Montreal.

Yet Marie-Hélène had invited him for Easter Sunday dinner. *You know how much it would mean to Danielle,* she'd said. *Please come.*

Arriving a few minutes early, he saw a car parked in front of the house, a stranger's. His wife was sitting beside the driver, no doubt a parishioner who'd brought her home from Mass. After a few minutes, she kissed him on both cheeks and they embraced. Pierre waited, until he realized that the man wasn't dropping her off. The two of them got out of the car and entered the house.

He felt an ache of sorrow, and then he thought about the despair that must have galled Marie-Hélène, forced to endure bouquets from his lover's niece, and he wondered at the dignity she'd summoned up in the simple act of receiving them. *C'est la justice,* he thought as he ran a comb through his hair, straightened his tie and gripped the box of chocolates his wife and daughter enjoyed. He went inside.

"How well you look," he told Marie-Hélène.

"*Merci.* It's because I'm happy." She introduced François, who was, indeed, a parishioner, one with no family of his own. At dinner, Pierre raised a glass to her long life.

Easter passed and May came, but Marie-Hélène didn't ask his help with the garden. "You've too much to plant as it is," she told him when she phoned, and he was surprised to feel a pang of disappointment.

She'd called to discuss separation.

"We are separate already," he said.

"There are papers to sign."

We haven't talked enough about this, he thought later. Perhaps as husband and wife, they'd never talked enough. Perhaps that was the whole point. One evening he called her.

"*Maman* is out," said Danielle. Her voice was sad.

"She's made a new friend, *oui?*" he asked.

"*Maman* says *la vie est brève.*"

"It's not about life being short," Pierre replied. "She's looking for hope."

Danielle didn't answer.

"*Moi, aussi,*" she said at last. "I am, too."

"Forgive me, *ma petite,*" he said. "These things happen in life sometimes."

Silence.

"I love you, Danielle."

The months faded into summer, and in August, a few weeks before Lorraine's arrival, he received a call from Marie-Hélène. She was going into the hospital for tests. He asked her what was wrong.

"Nothing," she replied.

All at once he felt afraid that he might lose her without having broken the hard rock of sorrow between them. He found himself asking what he could do for her, how he could be of help. When she replied that he shouldn't trouble himself, he thought he knew the reason. "Have you found love?" he asked.

"I've found distraction," she told him. "François is good company for now."

"You've found hope then."

"Yes, for now I've found hope," she answered.

He asked Marie-Hélène to call when she had news. "I'll only call if the news is good," she said.

"And if it's not?"

"I'll write," she told him.

Pierre groaned. "You take years to write letters, *ma chère*," he said.

On the south side of his cottage was a trellis heavy with fragrant roses. Pierre put on his garden gloves, cut a dozen with his shears, tied them with a red satin bow left over from Christmas and wrapped them in moist towels. On them he pinned a note: *Ma chère Marie-Hélène, with love and also, hope.* Then he drove into Montreal, and set the roses on her front porch. He didn't ring the bell, didn't check to see if a stranger's car was parked outside. He turned around and went back to the farm.

V

ON THE MORNING OF Lorraine's arrival, the air was hot and stormy, and Pierre went to the *dépanneur* for beer.

"*Tu as une lettre,*" said Gaetan. He reached into the cubbyhole. "Fresh today."

Pierre looked at the mail in his hand. He said nothing.

"You like your letters a week old, like the last one," said Gaetan. "Aged in wood."

"It came today?"

"*Vraiment,* as I said. If you don't want it, I'll feed it to the mice."

Pierre snatched the letter from his hand, shoved it in his pocket, strode off, forgot the beer. He slammed the door, then imagined Gaetan shaking his head, wondering what the hell was going on.

Pierre knew who the letter was from, but he hadn't time to read whatever troubling news it contained. Minutes after he returned home, he heard the crunch of wheels in his laneway. Drawing back the curtain, he watched Lorraine close the car door with care and silence, as if his farm and land were asleep and she was afraid of waking it.

He didn't run out to greet her, reluctant to hasten time that had moved with such lazy imprecision from their last encounter to now. A glimpse through the window told him that Lorraine was a fine-looking woman still, her thick caramel hair touched with gray. He could imagine her eyes alight with wit and cunning, her body ample and soft enough to bear the impact of some crushing blow in life. The end of their love, for example. She knocked and he opened the door.

"*Chère* Lorrie." He drew her inside and embraced her. When he let go, she stepped back, her look bemused.

"I have to tell you right off," she said, "that my French is gone, except for the odd word. I can follow you, though."

"Then I hope you don't mind if I speak French."

"*Bien entendu.* Nice digs you've got, Pierre. I see you've become a hippie."

No, he hadn't become a hippie, but he could feel her eyes resting in wonderment on his white hair, long and almost to his shoulders. He shrugged, then smiled at her. He had to get used to the bright twittering of a human voice, to the abrupt sense of motion in the room. It felt as if Lorraine were his host, plumping up pillows and tidying the house, trying to make him feel at home. Her words were an adornment to his austere place, like beadwork on rough linen. Bead upon bead, strings and swirls of leaving behind too much work, an ailing mother, a nice enough guy who was hot on her tail in Boston. She was taking a breather, driving through Maine and Vermont and right into Quebec, and my goodness, she'd never realized how quaint it was, all those church steeples and farms with pretty latticework gables and wooden swing-chairs — unbelievable, *la belle province,* granny country, its soft hills twinkling with ponds, their roundness dimpled with gravel roads. No pot, no hash, no messed-up kids. "Petey," she said, "What the hell are you doing in a place so nice?"

"It's quiet," he said.

"I'm talking too much, I take it. Never mind. I stopped at the *dépanneur* to get directions."

"Did Gaetan help you?"

Lorraine made a face. "You freaked him out, whatever you did this morning."

"I was in a hurry," said Pierre.

"He says you're *fou,* completely nuts. He warned me to be careful." She winked.

Pierre felt awkward, sure Lorraine could see his thoughts as they crouched behind his long and narrow face. It had been years, but he hoped he looked better than he did in the days when he'd been so cadaverous and ill. Yet not so long ago, Marie-Hélène had told him that he still looked haunted. She'd wondered at his spirit that would not relinquish the prisoner of war, his bones pressed against his skin, his clothes hanging loose from his body. Now he noticed that Lorraine's eyes were full of consternation, as if she saw this, also.

"You're well, Pierre?"

He told her he was well, yes.

She seemed at home with the mood of her surroundings, with his ancient pine table and chairs, his sofa covered with a crocheted afghan, a pair of snowshoes standing in the corridor. Over the fireplace was a rifle dressed with a sprig of Easter palm; above a doorway a crucifix. This might have been his *grand-père*'s house, his simple piety, his humble day and age. Pierre had kept these things the way they were when he bought the place from an old man years ago. He'd liked the mood of simplicity, a peace he'd felt reluctant to disturb. He reached out to the back of the couch and touched the afghan made by his wife, moving slowly as if he held an invisible cane in his hand.

"You see, I've grown old," he said.

"Come on. You're no older than I am."

He smiled. "I didn't say that you'd grown old." He could sense she felt aware of his gaze, a solitary man whose parched eyes absorbed her like rain.

He helped her unload her hamper. She'd brought jams and biscuits she'd made herself, along with some Boston treats, a bean-and-molasses casserole and sweet brown bread. Pierre stared at the array of foodstuffs on the table. He said *merci*, but he couldn't say any more. He wondered at her kindness as he picked up the jam jars one by one and held them up, jewel-like, to the light. In their reflection, he imagined the two of them as they might have been — a married couple, Lorrie stocking the kitchen of their home in Greenbanks because their daughter would be coming for the weekend with the grandchildren, *and we have to feed them, mon cher.* Or perhaps their child had been a boy, grown to manhood, a lawyer making his way in Boston, dropping by for Sunday dinner with a family of his own.

You have no right to imagine this, he thought.

"Lorrie, you are too kind," he said at last. He felt bewildered as he looked at the loaves of bread. "Who will eat all of this?"

Lorraine smiled. "You can freeze some of it," she told him, and she offered to put the food away. Pierre thanked her as he stood by the window, staring out at his fields, touching his breast pocket where the letter was.

While Lorraine took over his kitchen, Pierre read the note.

Pauvre Marie-Hélène, he thought.

Lorraine finished up, then turned to face him, her kind look dissolving into consternation. "Is everything all right, Pierre?" she asked.

He folded the note and put it back in his pocket. "I'll show you the farm," he said. "Come."

It wasn't much, he told her, only two hectares, most of which he didn't farm. He owned a barn and storage shed, the sugar-bush and the fields. He'd started a small apple orchard. Already he'd harvested the early crops — lettuce and spinach, radishes and peas — and the corn and tomatoes were ripening well in a long, warm summer. Lorraine admired the wildflowers growing at the edges of his fields, the thick spread of buttercups, daisies, chickory, Queen-Anne's-Lace, cow-vetch, and clover. Her praise reminded him of a card the girls made him on his birthday once. It showed *papa* dressed in a space suit, a pot of violets in his hand, a sign at his feet with the words *jardin lunaire*. Moon garden — how well they understood him, his kids.

As they walked by the new orchard, Pierre recalled the tree Allan planted one Arbor Day in Greenbanks, years ago. "I thought we might plant a sapling in his memory," he said to Lorraine. "I've been digging, you see."

He crouched down and picked up a handful of soil. Then he held it out to her. Instead of touching the rich loam, Lorraine clasped her hands around his. He let her; he felt in need of human warmth. For a moment he gazed at her in silence, the soil sifting down through his fingers, as if through some irreparable crack.

"It was good of you to come," he said.

"Danielle tells me it's been rough," she answered.

For a moment, Pierre didn't speak. "Danielle calls me *le jardinier sur la lune*," he said at last.

"Lost in space, moon-man. Well at least you've got a green thumb."

"It is hard to explain one's life to a child," he said.

"Have you tried?"

Pierre took a deep breath. "I cannot."

"Do you mean you'd rather not?"

"*Vraiment*, it is not your business."

"I'm sorry I asked. Give me that damn hoe, *carisse*." Lorraine began to loosen a clod of earth. The soil flew.

Pierre apologized for what he'd said. He explained that he and his wife had parted, and that he found it hard to be truthful with Danielle. Even harder had been the thought of talking to her sister Thérèse, who was older and more worldly. He explained that he'd been unable to speak to her through the blindness of the telephone, to confess to his first-born how he'd failed.

"Thérèse is much like me," he said. "She needs distance."

"Young people often do."

"Perhaps I've lost her."

A ghost she was, his Thérèse, like the air. He was losing his children.

"I think you're making more of it than you should," said Lorraine.

"Perhaps."

"Children grow up. If you love them, they come to understand."

Yes, in fact he did love his children, *grace à Dieu,* but in his heart he knew he'd been cruel to Marie-Hélène, humiliating her when she needed him most. Rather than say this, he told Lorraine that, not long ago, death had begun to wrench him apart from his wife. For weeks he hadn't eaten or slept, and the flesh of the two of them wasted together, hers from cancer and his from sorrow. Both of them knew that his ill health was buried trouble of another kind, and she'd asked him to leave her, that they both might recover. All this he told Lorraine, but not the harm he'd done that grieved him most.

He'd always wanted a chance to live alone, he said. He'd read Sartre after the war. *Enfer, c'est les autres.*

"I knew you were unhappy," said Lorraine. "But — *sheesh.*"

"Here for a *réunion,* you've come all this way for bad news."

She laughed. "Remember our toast, *to real life?*"

"When we parted, *oui,*" he answered.

Pierre offered to show her the back fields and the woodlot. Lorraine walked alongside him on the path, and he felt the breeze that picked up the folds of her dress, that tossed her hair in his face like lemon flowers.

"That toast sure was a hex," she said.

"You've had trouble, Lorrie?"

"One marriage, *x* number of boyfriends."

"A new guy chasing you in Boston, *oui*?" She looked pensive. He didn't dare ask about children.

"And then there's you," she said.

Lorraine turned to him and kissed him on the lips. He leaned against the trunk of a tree, feeling the soft pressure of her flesh against his body, the quick flick of her tongue in his mouth. She moved away and they walked back across the field in silence. Pierre felt shaken. He wished he hadn't allowed this. At the cottage, Lorraine fumbled around in the kitchen, preparing a lunch for their walk on the trail. She asked if there was anything he needed at the *dépanneur*. Pierre knew he'd forgotten the beer, and he mentioned some other things he didn't need at all. He felt relieved as she made her way to the door.

"Wait'll Gaetan sees me. Talk will fly," she said.

Pierre shrugged. "Let it."

"*Ce n'est pas ton truc*, gossip. It's not your thing, *oui*?"

"Lorrie, I have much on my mind."

"*Oui. Je comprends.*"

He let her go.

Pierre would not have told Lorraine that, as he felt her kiss, he looked up at the August sky and the war fell down on him. Once again he was among prisoners, hearing the racket of an approaching airlift, starving and desperate to be seen, tearing the rags from his body, ripping apart bedding for a huge white cross on the barracks roof. Down came the parachutes, weighted with boxes of meat and dried eggs, chocolate and biscuits. It felt like a wind-borne memory, and Lorrie was the wind.

In Greenbanks once again, he'd brought her sweets and flowers. It was 1945, and under his finger, a doorbell was about to ring. *Dear Lorrie, let's begin again,* he'd thought, sure his embrace would remind her how they'd slept together before he shipped out to the Philippines, years before the war had ravaged everything. As a soldier, that memory had sustained him until he was taken prisoner. Years later, still locked inside himself, he wished he could ring that doorbell once again. *Lorrie, somewhere in the world there's a child we never mention, a moment between us of innocence and sorrow that took on flesh and lived. Now time has blown you back to me. Maybe it's time to understand what happened.*

Could he have picked a worse time?

He opened the letter he'd carried all day in his pocket, and he read it again. *The cancer has returned, but I am not without hope. My brother has explained to me that there are matters we must settle just in case. It would be prudent if you would come to Montreal.*

Hope he would have to gather with all the strength he had. He would talk to Lorrie and tell her about the letter when they went for their hike. First he'd call Marie-Hélène and tell her he'd come tonight. He glanced at a sky that threatened rain, remembering how he brought her roses. He hoped there'd be time enough to help her. Whatever would help, he'd do. Yet this battle was one of extravagance, cacophony, the noise of rescue, a largeness he wasn't sure he possessed. He'd have to run to the moon and pick her an armful of wildflowers, fill up a basket with the bread that rained from heaven, grab God by the scruff of the neck and scream in his face. He wasn't sure he could. Yet at least he wouldn't run away from her. Solace and comfort, that much he could give.

VI

THREE YEARS AGO, ON the night before her surgery, Marie-Hélène had taken his face in her hands so that he could see the serenity of her gaze. *Mon Dieu,* he thought — there was no need for so much bravery. "But that was how my parents made it through the war," she said. "When the Germans occupied Paris." Ovarian cancer. He'd been afraid of this enemy's stealth, but so was she, he felt certain. Yet he wondered how it was that two people married for years, intimate in bed, their bodies hiding nothing, could nonetheless hide from each other how terrified they were.

"*Prends courage,* Pierre, I will be fine."

"You are brave, *ma chère.*"

She'd looked perplexed. "And you are not?"

"I am not."

Marie-Hélène had patted his cheek. "You're too modest, *un vrai canadien,*" she'd said. "You've forgotten the war."

Pierre strode over to the closet and found her suitcase. It was small, and with a quick yank, he'd pulled it down from the shelf, knocking over a hatbox, a shawl, a sewing basket. Out fell a spray of pins and needles, a cat's tangle of yarn and thread. He'd crouched down and begun picking everything up.

"I'll help you pack, if you like," he said.

"*Ce n'est pas nécessaire.*" She'd folded her arms and watched him.

"I'm being clumsy."

"Leave it, Pierre. I'll fix it."

"Get some rest, then."

"Pierre," she'd said, "your courage gives me strength."

He'd taken her hands and kissed them. He would come to bed soon, he said. *Bonne nuit, ma chère*, and he'd gone to his study and leaned against the wall, imagining that with his strength he could support the stonework on the outer walls as well, brace the joists that held up the ceiling, keep the roof, the whole house from crashing in on him.

Danielle made supper the following evening. Pierre was touched by the familiar smells of *soupe des legumes*, roasted chicken, homemade bread. He tried the soup, thanked her, told her he wasn't very hungry. "*Ils ont du succès avec ça,*" he explained to her, meaning the surgery, meaning whatever success could be chipped away from a stone-hard case like her mother's. Five years of life? Ten? He had no idea. He broke off a piece of bread, buttered it, took a bite, put it down.

"When your mother recovers, I'll take her on a trip," he told his daughter.

Her eyes widened. "California?"

"France. To see her cousins."

"You should take *maman* to see Thérèse."

He knew that Danielle missed her big sister, her sophistication and good English. Thérèse had sent photos of herself in the beautiful tie-dyed silks she made, sitting in front of her Victorian house on Haight Street. Her smile was blissful enough to concern her father. *J'espère qu'elle ne se drogue pas,* he'd thought, but Danielle felt certain she wasn't doing drugs.

Once Pierre had walked by her room and glimpsed his youngest daughter practising English phrases, her text in one hand, a photo of her sister in the other. Danielle was addressing the photo, the drift of an accent in her voice, and she made him think of a child eating ice cream, her tongue lost in the sweet, delicious spiral of the cone. *My sister lives in San Francisco, where there are palm trees and eucalyptus. I would like to see the Golden Gate Bridge.* Then she'd kissed the photo of Thérèse goodnight, continuing to read in the lost tongue of her father. Watching her, he'd felt old and in exile, surprised by his grief. Now he looked at Danielle again.

"Thérèse we'll visit, *oui,*" he'd said.

"*Je lui écris en anglais.* I write to her in English," she'd replied. "She says that Americans — "

"*En français, s'il vous plaît.* Speak French."

"*Papa, vraiment —* "

It was hopeless to argue, her look said. Danielle and Thérèse had both studied English because it was American and glamorous and happened to be the language of their father's secrets. *Papa, why won't you speak to us in English?* Danielle would say.

Ours is a French home, he'd answer. *Isn't there enough English spoken in Montreal? You learn it in school. You can pick it up on the street. We have to draw a line somewhere.*

Given the times, he'd assumed that his two girls would turn out to be radicals, French-only separatists, proud of his unilingual stand. Now he wondered why they had to go and be different from all their hippie friends who tore the city apart on Jean-Baptiste Day, who went to *manifestations* and waved placards, who painted the fleur-de-lys on their faces.

Because he wouldn't talk to them, that's why.

Danielle had started to clear the dishes. He told her to leave them, that she should do her homework. Alone he put away the rest of the food and began scraping the plates. Crumbs, scraps of meat on bones, a meal's worth once. *Take it, Pete. Go on,* Allan had said. English words — he knew he mustn't blame Danielle, poor child, for stirring this in him, but he'd like to take *anglais* and stuff it in the trash, and here she'd set it loose in the house like vermin. He glanced at the bones on her plate. Once he'd taken food from a dying man, gnawing at it like a rat. He'd wanted to live, to go home to Lorraine. He had to forget this.

Danielle, parles français.

A year after the surgery, Marie-Hélène recovered, and in the fall of 1969, Pierre took her to France. The pleasant trip exhausted her. She'd told Pierre he mustn't worry, that it was only the fatigue of travel. Yet he'd been frightened, sure the surgery hadn't helped. A storm of cancer cells was tearing her apart; of course that must be it. Untroubled, Marie-Hélène rested at home, enjoying visits from her two sisters and her friends from church who helped with chores and meals. Pierre couldn't sleep, couldn't eat.

One evening he'd gotten drunk. He'd gone outside, tearing into his garden, ripping out shrubbery and his reckless patch of flowers. He couldn't explain why he'd done this. Marie-Hélène had been outraged. Remorseful, he'd apologized and promised to replace the hedge. The wildflowers returned without his help, in their mad profusion of grace.

Yet Pierre couldn't name what had broken in him. It felt as if the still centre of his life lay in ruins. He'd go to the washroom and be ill, leaving others to assure Marie-Hélène: family, acquaintances, the mothers or aunts of children to whom she'd taught piano. Nicole's niece would arrive for her lesson with a small bouquet for Madame LeBlanc, a gift to console her in the long night of a Montreal winter. She was elusive, Nicole, and her presence made him feel desperate, as if he were trapped in death and she were his only hope of rescue. Unable to sleep, he told Marie-Hélène that he didn't want to disturb her rest. He slept in his study, imagining Nicole in his arms.

Marie-Hélène had to go for post-operative tests. "Be calm," she'd said to Pierre. "I don't want you ruining the garden once again."

Pierre had felt no better as the new year came, as winter turned to spring. Almost two years after the surgery, his wife appeared to be doing well. Yet nothing could allay his fear, and only the tight clamp of daily routine could hold his life together. Every day before work, he'd pay a visit to a *dépanneur* near his office, then take his coffee and a croissant to a sidewalk table where he'd read the paper. A glance at his watch allowed him to note the half hour that would have elapsed from the time he'd made his purchases to the folding of a serviette before he'd crush his refuse in his fist, shove it into the trash and stride the few blocks to his office at the ministry. He'd try not to think about Marie-Hélène, her doctors' appointments, her rounds of tests. Instead he'd live his careful measuring out of life as if it were rationed, as if it were the only way to make it last.

One morning the headline in his paper read: *Pour Les Soldats Perdus, La Guerre N'est Pas Finie.* For Missing Soldiers, the War Isn't Over. These men were Japanese who'd been in hiding in some Asian jungle, who'd just been told that the Second World War had ended years ago, who'd feared surrender and disgrace. *C'est vraiment juste*, Pierre had thought. *Like prison. They should make them stay there.* He'd picked up the paper and folded it in quarters, slipping it in the pocket of his raincoat. Later at work, he'd pulled it out and read the foreboding article again. The newsprint blurred, gray and soft in his hands.

As he left work and strode toward the Métro, Pierre remembered that he still had the paper. He tossed it in the garbage, glancing up to see a bearded man in jeans about to enter the subway, his arm around a young woman the same age as Danielle, a pretty girl with a bolt of lustrous hair. She was wearing sandals and a long, printed dress; her *chum* had an American flag stitched upside-down on the seat of his pants. Pierre shuddered, as if his act of discarding the paper had caused these phantoms from his homeland to appear in front of him. *Les américains qui parlent français.* Fluent in French —

some Americans were. It was possible. As the couple made their way down the stairs, they seemed to evaporate into darkness. It was, he thought, an omen, and he'd felt afraid.

He rode the Métro, got off at Place d'Armes, walked east until he found the laneway that led to Nicole's flower shop. It was a modest place, almost lost in the shadows of ancient buildings darkening the street. There was a sign *Fermé* outside, but Nicole was there, and Pierre eyed the window until she turned around and saw him. She came and opened the door.

"It's all right, Pierre. I'll open."

He told Nicole he wanted flowers for Marie-Hélène, and he saw a pot of hyacinths, the smell of them so intense that his tongue could taste their gemlike beauty, their bright, sweet plum liqueur. It must have been then that it broke inside of him — the power of the mysterious place he'd called his marriage, its cloister of serenity, its end of terror. Why peace chose to flee in that intense color breaking on his tongue, he didn't know. Only that once again he was standing on the shore, watching the flotsam of his life as it was swept out to sea. Once again a hurricane was smashing the sea wall into a shrieking gull's cacophony of tongues. *Les deux jeunes* had been speaking English, not French, and the young man wore the American flag upside-down as a signal of distress. What war? What year? He felt the ground-thudding shake of a bomb, saw in the tankers of Manila Bay the light of a vast and terrible explosion.

The paper he'd tossed in the garbage, that headline.

"What would you like, Pierre?"

"Je voudrais ces fleurs-là." He indicated the flowers, aware that he felt afraid and didn't know why. Nicole looked almost luminous, like an x-ray held up to light, her denim jacket, short skirt and blouse aglow. Her thick blonde hair was translucent, beautiful, almost white, her eyes ebbing into a tide of blackness. He thought of radiation, as if her body was matter in decay, as if this woman were the frail spirit of Marie-Hélène. Flesh and bone and human names — all of them illusions, as if he could reach through Nicole and into the heart of matter and its dreadful, radiant light.

His hand was shaking as he went to pay her and he dropped his change on the counter. Nicole put her hand on his. Gesturing for him to follow her, she walked up a flight of stairs, her eyes lowered, her head drooping like a tulip half-broken on its stem. She must have known she was flotsam, about to be crushed by a tidal wave of desperation, his.

Worse, he'd known that he'd do nothing to stop this.

He turned her around and pressed her against the wall, pushing his tongue into her mouth and fondling her. The world tipped sideways, spilling him like rain, bending his soul as light bends in the pull of gravity. He'd be ground to dust by the weight of what he was doing. His eyes were full of tears.

"What is it?" she asked.

"You mustn't love me," he answered.

"You always say that."

"How often have I come?"

She smiled. "Often enough."

When was it he'd seen the man with the distress-flag, the woman with the tie-dyed dress, that headline in the paper? Today? A month ago? Time was water, drowning him.

He took the hyacinths and left.

Pierre returned home, gave the flowers to Marie-Hélène, and the war continued, floating dead under the still, transparent surface of the world. He'd fallen ill and couldn't sleep. *Our Father who art in heaven. Forgive us.* Yet he went back to Nicole again and again, confessing that he hated himself for his infidelity and weakness, until at last Nicole confronted him. *I won't have you using me to prove that you're a liar and a coward,* she said. Their liaison ended then.

One night Marie-Hélène asked him, as she'd done years ago, if he could live alone again.

"If I had to, yes," he answered.

"I have watched you for a while now," she began. "You and Nicole."

He said nothing.

"It is true then?"

"It is over," he replied.

"Pierre," she continued, "I am going to ask you to leave me."

"But you're ill," he said.

Her eyes were troubled as she lay back on the pillows. "You must leave so that I may get well," she said. Those had been her words, not *because you were unfaithful.* He knelt by her side, and taking her hand, he held it to his lips. What dignity, that she allowed him this gesture after so much lying and deceit.

"I can't lose you, Marie-Hélène," he'd said.

Her eyes met his. "You're afraid of my illness, aren't you?"

He nodded.

"Go find courage. In a few months we will talk."

That night, he dreamt he'd seen a Japanese hiding in a ravine, concealed by knotted brush, a place gouged out of alluvial slopes that followed Mount Bataan to Manila Bay, Corregidor and the sea. The man was a soldier forced to trudge his way through malarial swamps, surviving on rice husks and the innards of dogs, washing his body in a fetid stream. This was his hell, his punishment: never to leave here. He'd heard a soldier accusing the man, and then he'd realized the soldier's voice was his own. *You will never again find hearth or abode. You are going to die alone, an object of scorn and ridicule, never again to see your children or to hold your wife in bed.*

The following morning, he'd told Marie-Hélène that he'd go.

It was a year since they'd parted.

Lost in memory, Pierre opened Marie-Hélène's letter and read it again. *I will come if you wish,* he would say to his wife.

Very good, she'd reply. *We can go over our documents. Pierre?*

Oui? He imagined their voices, their wintry sound, like the scrape of icy branches on glass.

Let us forgive each other, she'd say.

No, it was he who needed forgiving, not her. *Please forgive me, Marie-Hélène. Even if we never reconcile. Even if you find love.*

He walked to the orchard. Remembering the tree they meant to plant for Lorrie's brother, he found a shovel and began to dig a hole. Once again he was digging in memory, burying flesh as gray and bloated as rotting fruit. *Non, pas encore.* He thrust the shovel in the ground, left it there and walked away. *Poor Marie-Hélène,* he thought. *She will have a more peaceful end than Alain and his buddies.*

Pierre turned around, walked back to the orchard and stared at what he'd begun. He knew he couldn't turn his back forever on this shovel, this hole in the ground. He was going to have to make his peace with death, with the scythe in the long grass.

VII

STILL PONDERING THE LETTER, Pierre went back to the house and tried to call Marie-Hélène. He got a busy signal, and then he put off calling her while he fumbled around the kitchen, packing provisions for their hike — rain-slickers, water and sandwiches, fruit and some candy bars Danielle had given him. *Ces tablettes de granola sont organiques,* she told her father. He thought they looked like cattle feed, and he welcomed the distraction of pondering kids who ate tofu and bean sprouts, who avoided the pleasures of alcohol. *Alain, how much has changed since we signed that note. Thirty years have gone to dust.* Recalling his buddy, he packed a flask of rye, sure they'd get around to toasting his memory. He wondered where Lorraine was. He imagined Gaetan's tart and silly flirting, Lorrie making a rude joke. How he wished for life, abundant and careless as this. He stared at the phone.

When he'd run out of reasons to procrastinate, he called again. Danielle answered and told him what she could, saying that Marie-Hélène was resting. He called the specialist in Montreal. While he was on the phone, he heard the door open. Lorraine was carrying her bundles into the kitchen, her face grave, as if she'd been listening to his conversation. He finished his call, went to help her, found her pouring rye into a glass. She handed it to him.

"*Bien*, you are kind," he said.

"I hope you'll forgive me for this morning."

It seemed days ago, that kiss. He looked at the letter in his hand. "My wife hasn't long," he told her.

"I'm sorry, Pierre."

"Danielle doesn't know this. Neither does Marie-Hélène. But her doctor wants to see the two of us. In person." He gulped down his drink and banged his glass on the table. Then he turned his back to her and hid his face in his hands. Marie-Hélène had been too exhausted to come to the phone, too busy preparing to leave this world. Even if she forgave him, she couldn't reconcile him to her going.

"I know how this feels," said Lorraine.

Pierre looked up. "*Vraiment*, we are here because you do," he answered. He slipped on his backpack. "*Allons*," he said. "Let's go."

They set out along the trail that began on the edge of his woodlot. It wound uphill to an overlook into the valley, a rocky spot where the roots of conifers made gnarled steps that spiralled upward. He let Lorraine take his arm as she climbed. It had been a long time since she'd done this, and in her touch Pierre felt the flight of another twenty years, as if he were already an elderly man with a hesitant step and a frail arm to hold. He'd always thought that by the time a man turned seventy, he'd feel that each touch echoed and contained all of the others. Yet long ago, he'd sent his memory of his youth into exile. At the age of fifty, he felt as if he'd always been old, a man who'd forgotten much, who refused to remember anything.

They hiked in silence, grabbing each other's hands and the trunks of trees, climbing past boulders and slopes to level ground. Then the trail began to grow silent, as if its thick beds of pine needles cushioned and absorbed sound. There was no wind, no rustling of leaves or bird-song. The air began to feel warmer and more humid, as heavy as a coat he couldn't remove. Pierre walked to an outcropping of rock that overlooked the valley. On his face he felt rain.

"*Enfin*," he said. "Showers."

He gazed at a tangled slide of scrub-brush and grasses below them. The fine drizzle made the earth look gray. He could see farms, half-hidden in a blister of fog. The light was as pale as watery milk, as if he were afflicted with cataracts and could no longer see the world as it was. Here and there were colours in the gray, the dazzle of flowers that haunted his gardens. He pointed down.

"You see my orchard," he said.

He pulled out the flask of rye, opened it and passed it to her. They both drank as they stared at the row of saplings, at a small hole filling up with water.

"Is that for Allan's tree?" she asked.

"*Oui.* I started the hole."

It seemed he'd never stopped digging, as if he were condemned to live with his foot on the edge of a shovel, his weight forever pushing it into the ground. He drank again and passed her the flask.

"This morning I thought of Alain," he said.

"*Oui. Moi, aussi.*"

"And Marie-Hélène. Soon I will bury her also."

"I am sorry," she said. She passed the flask back to him.

Pierre looked away. *Let us lift a glass to those who know what's what, who are forced to shovel dirt on their buddies' corpses. Let us raise a glass to the lid slamming shut on our fingers. Let us, let us.* He lifted the flask and turned to her.

"Let us toast the end of the fucking world," he said in English.

He was about to hurl the flask down on the rocks when Lorraine grabbed his arm, yanked it back, pulled the bottle out of his hand and shoved it in her pocket. "Goddammit, Pete," she said, and he could feel her drawing him close, taking him in her arms. Her warmth was unbearable, a comfort that made him feel weak and close to death. No, he'd betrayed her once before, and he couldn't go back to his youth, to the moment before his world collapsed. He pushed her away and turned his back to her.

"Lorrie, I can't," he said.

"Can't what? Hug me?"

Pierre remembered her kiss. "You know what would follow," he said.

"You should be so lucky."

"Lorrie, I —"

"And I'm too old to get knocked up."

He was shocked into silence — shocked enough to imagine for the first time his beloved Lorrie when she was young, desperate to find a way out of trouble.

"I'm not so damn stupid as you think," she said.

"Nor I," he whispered, but images assaulted him — Lorrie slamming her fists into her stomach, dousing herself with herbs and potions, thinking she might throw herself down the fire escape in back of her parents' apartment. He felt remorseful, that he'd never dwelled on her suffering. *And why not?* he wondered.

Because he'd been dogged by shadows dragging themselves in a ragged line on the march out of Bataan and because in that bloody spring of 1942 he hadn't the heart to think about Lorraine's predicament. At the time she was facing birth alone, he was standing in terror, watching buddies pulled out of the line and shot. He was waiting his turn, one of three hundred innocent men who would never see their children.

How clever the mind can get with words, he thought. *Excuses.*

Not shot. Beheaded.

The Japanese passed over him, taking the soldiers on his right and left.

He lost her then.

VIII

LORRAINE GLARED AT HIM, then turned around and strode off down the path, the way they'd come. At that moment, it began to pour. Pierre was alarmed, splattered with mud as he made his way down the side of the hill after her.

"Lorrie — "

"*Quoi?*"

"You cannot climb downhill alone in the rain." He grabbed her arm and pulled her into a shelter, a rock outcropping that formed a cave. She pulled away.

"Lorrie, I'm sorry," he said. "I have never told you — "

" — what planet you come from. So tell me."

Her face looked weary, as it had the day he'd returned to her from the war, and Pierre felt sure that life was giving him a chance to set things right, to break through the silence that imprisoned both of them. He imagined himself young and more courageous, ringing the doorbell of Lorraine's house. In his head, he heard her voice from years ago: *There's nothing to say*. This time, he'd challenge that. This time, there'd be plenty to say.

"I have never told you much," he said.

"That's for sure."

"Or insisted on you telling me."

She paused. "I put a finger to your lips," she answered.

He took her hands. "As if we were young, as if I had just come home, *dis-moi*," he whispered. "Tell me what happened."

Lorraine looked taken aback. "What, to the child?"

"*Oui*."

She was silent at first, as if she had to retrieve the answer from a deep well of memory.

"I saw to it," she said, "that there was no child."

"I don't understand," he said, and then he did. He dropped her hands. "*C'est pas vrai*," he said.

"It's the truth."

He turned his back and hid his face from her. How slowly time moved then, and his body felt leaden, as if he were dreaming, trying to run in terror. He'd never considered that Lorraine might have been that desperate. He was too selfish to allow her suffering to live in his mind because he'd wanted to believe that their single moment of happiness had taken on flesh and was still alive in the world, and he turned toward Lorraine, hearing her fading voice as thin and distant as a telephone call from overseas. *Petey, you said you wanted to know.*

Yet it had taken him thirty years of travel to cross this wilderness of grief between them, and so he put his arms around her and wept into her hair. In his arms was silence; to silence he was condemned. He could still hear Allan's words:

She's going to have a kid, Pete. For Chrissakes, be a man and write to her, and his answer. *What the hell, we're all going to die here.* A week later the Japanese destroyed Bataan.

Even so.

"Lorrie, *pardonne-moi*."

"For what?"

Pierre didn't answer, didn't tell her why he wanted forgiveness. He couldn't meet her eyes.

Caught in the rain, they sat under the rock ledge and Lorraine told him only that she'd found her way to New York City. She'd never returned there, not even for a visit. "What I've done, I've done," she said, and then she said no more about it. Pain and the ghost of their youth spilling over the edges of memory, down into toilets, sewers, city drains; the thought filled Pierre with grief.

And what if long ago we'd spoken, what if she'd never put a finger to my lips, what if I'd never raised a glass to real life, to what's what, *to everything that crushed us?* He felt grieved and spent and as old as *grand-père's* harrow-blade in the hard soil.

"What we have lived through," he said.

"More than enough," she answered.

Pierre opened his pack, pulled out a sandwich, gave half of it to Lorraine. She asked him to tell her about Bataan, and he tried, but he couldn't find the words. They had gone too deep into him or too far away from him; they were terrible and holy, a place where he knelt. "My friends are buried there," he said. He thought of Marie-Hélène, waiting her turn, and he reached out to the quiet rain that wept on a solitary hand.

"I'm going to Montreal tonight." Pierre took the flask from Lorraine and raised it. "To fortune," he said.

They drank the last of the rye. Down came a cloudburst, one of cataracts and fertile riverbanks, punching and slapping as it beat the earth and wept on stony ground, as it fell on his crops with grace.

"One more round," said Lorrie.

Pierre set the empty flask outside the overhang of rock until the water filled it. In Allan's memory, they drank the rain.

Acknowledgements

I would like to thank Quattro Books for their kind support of my work through the Ken Klonsky Novella Contest. Special thanks to John Calabro for a thoughtful and insightful reading and editing of this manuscript. I am grateful to the Ontario Arts Council for their generous financial contribution to this project. And *merci*, Brian — first reader, spouse and friend. May your garden bloom.

Ken Klonsky Novella Contest